The River Guardian is released with authorisation from Insomnia Knights Productions, Nottingham, England

Full colour illustrations available upon request by contacting the author at:

authordamienbrough@gmail.com

Follow the author on Facebook and Twitter at:

@Damienbrough1

This book is dedicated to all the people that have helped make it happen over the years.

To Sarah for your unwavering support.

To Dan for joining me on this journey.

And to all the other people who have helped and supported me on this dream, there are too many to name but please know that I have appreciated everything that you all have done for me.

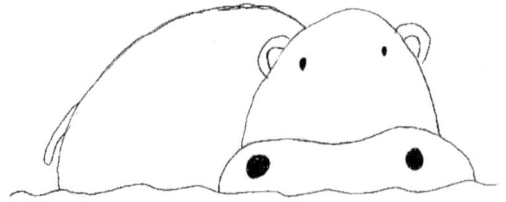

Hippopotamus has a bad day

I want to tell you a story, a story about the Hippopotamus
and how he became the guardian of the river. He wasn't
always the big protector that he is today and he didn't
always spend his days swimming in the mighty river. In
fact, our story begins as so many do, with our hero actually
being the villain of his own story.

The days of the Hippopotamus were simple, he would wake
up whenever he wanted, eat whatever he wanted, bully
whomever he wanted and then after an afternoon nap, he

would eat whatever he wanted again and then go back to sleep whenever he wanted. To the mighty Hippopotamus life was good, however, there are always two sides to every story and for all the other animals' life with Hippopotamus was never very fun at all.

Imagine waking up and trying to get your breakfast not knowing when a big scary Hippopotamus would come along and snatch your food or if whenever you wanted to play a game you knew the Hippopotamus would trample in and take over or at the very least make you feel small and weak as he started to bully everyone. The only time the animals felt like they could be animals at all was during the Hippopotamus's afternoon nap and even then, they had to be quiet so as not to wake or anger him. Even the mighty lion, the king of the jungle, knew to fear an angry Hippopotamus because even his sharp teeth and long claws were not enough to hurt the mighty creature. He could charge like a rhino, stomp like an elephant and could pull you under the water like an alligator, and so all the animals did their best to stay away from him. Just like most bullies however, Hippopotamus thought he was popular and that he was only having a little bit of fun with all the other animals. He could not see that what he was doing was hurting them and scaring them and driving them away.

"It's all a bit of fun" he would say to himself, "just a game" he would call out reassuringly not realising that it was he himself that he was trying to reassure and just like most bullies this was enough to convince himself that he wasn't really bad at all. One morning after he had, as he put it, 'shared' the young lion cubs' breakfast, that their mother had hunted for them, he set off down to the lake for a nice long drink of refreshingly cool water. When he arrived, he saw a group of young deer playing in the lake, they were joyfully splashing around and kicking water at each other and jumping on each other's backs all the while laughing together.

The mighty Hippopotamus saw this and immediately

started to charge down to the water's edge bellowing out

his deep Hippopotamus laugh. As he approached the water

the deer froze, each of them looking around for the cause of

all the noise but by the time they had spotted him it was too

late. The roaring hippopotamus barged through them,

knocking them this way and that and as he reached the edge

of the water, he jumped towards a group of swimming deer

landing right in the middle of them laughing as he splashed

and thrashed about amongst the group.

The deer all swam for the shore and ran off up the hill

leaving him behind. Happy that he had won the game he

took a big drink of water and sauntered off up the hill

towards a large tree where he lay down in the shade and let

his mind wander back to the fun he'd had and quickly

found himself falling to sleep.

It was a little after noon when Hippopotamus awoke from his slumber. After a quick stretch and a long yawn, he nipped back down to the lake for another drink. When he arrived he saw all the deer standing there, looking into the lake. Not moving. Just looking. Impatient, as he always was, he pushed through the crowd to get to the water's edge so that he could get his drink and to see what all the fuss was about. As he reached the edge, he saw one of the elder bucks in the water dragging something out and waded in for a closer look. It was one of the youngest fawns that had been playing earlier, except he was no longer playing, he had died.

"You did this" he heard crying out behind him. "You killed our baby" cried the fawns' mother from the front of the group.

"Quiet" hissed the buck in the water "we don't know what happened".

"Yes, we do" she sobbed back "all the younglings saw it, he charged through them and pounced on our baby".

Hippopotamus was dumbfounded. All he had done was come for a drink and now he was being accused of this. "I... I..." he tried to talk but was immediately interrupted.

"See, he has no words for what he has done" the mother cried out.

"I..." Hippopotamus tried again.

"He's not even sorry" came a shout from the crowd.

"He was laughing when he did it" called one of the fawns.

"I..." he tried again but was quickly cut off.

"He has always been like this" another voice shouted from the back of the crowd. "He doesn't care about anything but himself" the shouts continued. Every time Hippopotamus tried to speak up another member of the group would just shout him down. Until he eventually screamed out.

"FINE" his booming voice echoed around the whole lake, which startled the deer, causing them all to fall silent and back away from him. "Think whatever you want" he continued "I don't care" and with that he stomped his way back up the hill and back behind his tree.

The rest of the day was spent grumbling about how the deer had lied about him and about how they had gotten him wrong. They had been jumping on each other before he got there.

The day had turned to night and he had become very tired but he now knew what had happened, they had killed the young fawn and were trying to blame him so that they didn't get into trouble. He wanted to go and tell the group what had happened but it was too late and he was tired so he closed his eyes and quickly fell asleep.

As the morning sun rose, Hippopotamus quickly got up and knew what he needed to do. Off he went towards the deer's home on the other side of the plains. First, he ran past the lion cubs having their breakfast but he didn't notice them trying to hide their food. Next, he ran through the trees and all the birds took flight and finally he crossed the plains and ran into the home of the deer. However, when he arrived there was no one there.

"They left yesterday" a soft voice hissed from under one of the bushes. "They packed up after they had buried one of their children" the voice hissed again as a puff adder slithered out into view. "They blamed you" he said with a wry little smile "said you killed the fawn; said you were laughing whilst you did".

"I did nothing wrong" shouted Hippopotamus "it was them, the other deer, they killed the fawn and not me". His shouts changed to a softer whimper "They are lying about me".

"Doesn't matter really, they are gone and no one is going to believe you, no one ever believes a bully like you" and with his final word hissed, the adder slithered back under his bush and disappeared through the tall grass.

"They have to listen" Hippopotamus shouted to himself "I'll make them listen." Off he went back towards the lake and back towards anyone that might listen. First, he ran through the trees shouting his innocence but the birds just flew away, this time however, he could hear them calling to each other.

"Careful, stay away or he'll get you too". Then he ran into the open, towards where the cubs had been but as he arrived, he was met by the full pride of lions.

"Keep running murderer" they growled at him. "Animals don't kill for fun". He tried to stop to talk to them but they began to snarl and growl. "GO" they shouted and Hippopotamus knew they would not listen so off he ran. After reaching the lake he saw the alligators on the far side and he began to run around to them but as they saw him approaching, they started to swim towards the centre of the lake.

"You can't jump on us" they shouted; "We can swim away" and with that they all dove under the water and swam away. Through the rest of the day Hippopotamus would chase down the other animals and try to convince them of his innocence, but one by one they called him a liar and a murderer. Even the predators would have nothing to do with him and so off he went back to his tree and after a big drink from the lake he settled down and went back to sleep.

The following day was the same. Every time he ran towards someone, they either ran or called him murderer and as he searched for someone, anyone that believed him, another day was gone and it was getting too late for him to find his way back to his tree.

As the night fell and everything around him became dark, he began to hear strange noises. Weird animals that he had never seen before were flying all around him flapping, clicking and chirping overhead and not letting him sleep. As he listened the chirping sounds became words. "Killer" and "monster" filled the night's sky and Hippopotamus started to cry but these were not tears of sadness. There was no sobbing, his sadness had been replaced, with a hatred for the other animals.

The next few days were simple for Hippopotamus, he woke up when he wanted, ate whatever he wanted, bullied whomever he wanted and then after an afternoon nap, he ate whatever he wanted again and then went to sleep whenever and wherever he wanted. Day after day he got angrier and angrier. Each day he got meaner and meaner towards the other animals and so they began to stay away because none of them wanted to deal with an angry Hippopotamus. Further and further he went until he was so far from his tree and his favourite lake that he had begun to forget about them, so far in fact that the animals he came across no longer knew about the fawn in the lake. But this did not matter to Hippopotamus, not now, not anymore. Why should he care what the other animals thought, they were all the same to him.

Hippopotamus lived alone and ate alone, he played alone and slept alone and after a while this is how he thought he wanted to live. Alone. Each time another animal would move near to him he would at first try to scare them away and if that failed, he would just move again until he was alone. As he moved further away however he found that he wasn't finding somewhere to be alone but rather that the animals that he did find were just a little different. There were fewer lions and deer, and he hadn't seen a giraffe in a long while but he had met leopards and panthers hiding in the trees as well as monkeys. Hippopotamus hated the monkeys most of all as they used to hide in the trees and throw things at him as he walked past or when he tried to sleep.

One night as Hippopotamus was just falling asleep beside a large tree the monkeys started to laugh again. And with their laughter came the throwing of nuts and sticks that they had pulled from the tree. As they pelted him, he got up, and with an angry roar like shout he charged the tree and all the monkeys began to slip. One by one they leapt down from the higher branches and they swung across from tree to tree until they were out of sight. Fed up with them and angry

that they dared attack him, Hippopotamus began to chase

them through the trees until he came across a clearing.

Having lost the monkeys, he decided that this was as good

a spot as any to get some sleep and dropped down next to

one of the larger trees and tried to sleep. But before he

could even close his eyes, he heard the sound of laughter

again but this time it wasn't accompanied by throwing but

rather by the sound of singing and music.

Curiosity got the best of him and he walked up to the top of a nearby hill and as he looked down, he could see a bright light dancing in the middle of a group of oddly shaped caves and around the light danced a group of animals that Hippopotamus had never seen before. As Hippopotamus neared these new animals, he began to notice that they resembled the monkeys that had been throwing things at him. But unlike those monkeys these animals did not hide in the trees, instead, they seemed to live in the small caves around the fire. He also noticed that they were covered in a lot less fur. He walked ever closer trying not to be seen, which for a giant Hippopotamus isn't an easy task. A Hippopotamus hiding behind a tree is not a hiding Hippopotamus after all.

The trouble with curiosity

Curiosity can be a good thing; Going out and discovering

something new and exciting, making new friends, trying

new things. The world is a wonderful place. However,

when you are an angry Hippopotamus, curiosity can get

you in a lot of trouble.

Managing to reach the outside of the ring of caves he

noticed how truly odd they looked, almost like they were

not natural and they started to move when he accidentally

bumped into one. This alerted the animals to his presence and the dancing soon stopped. Realising that he had been seen Hippopotamus decided now was the time to scare these new animals away and with a mighty roar he charged out from behind the cave and ran towards the light that was still dancing in the middle of the now stunned group. Unlike the other animals however, these new creatures did not flee. They seemed as curious as Hippopotamus had been and so they stood their ground. Hippopotamus was a little shocked by this; everyone ran from him, the monkeys ran, the deer ran, even the mighty lions used to run away from the mighty Hippopotamus, but not these animals. So, he roared again but still they did not run, he took a step closer and roared again, followed by another, then another until he was close enough to one of the creatures to reach out and touch it.

Now this is the moment that if Hippopotamus wasn't so angry, he might have just made a new friend but unfortunately for Hippopotamus he was always angry, always sure that no one would want to be his friend so he did not take this chance to try. Instead, he decided to give the closest animal a quick nudge to show them that they should be scared of him. This did not have the effect that Hippopotamus had expected. Once he had hit the closest member of the group the little creature went flying through the air and all the other animals just looked on for a few seconds before they all started to run to their caves, but just as Hippopotamus was beginning to feel good about scaring them off, they all came back out with long pointed sticks in one hand and big pieces of wood in the other. The first of the group to reach the side of the light pointed the end of his stick at Hippopotamus and he was soon joined by all the others. They started roaring themselves and began lunging forwards with their out stretched sticks. The roars turned to shrieks as they approached. It was obvious to Hippopotamus that these little creatures were trying to scare him away. No one scared the mighty Hippopotamus though, and so he began to roar again, this time so loud that he hurt his own throat. He pushed forwards with all his might and began to charge at the group, however, he had not anticipated how sharp and pointy their sticks were and was soon shouting in pain as much as he was in anger. This did not stop him though, it just made him angrier and angrier until he was so mad that he didn't care about the pain anymore. He ran straight through them all and even ran through the dancing light stopping it from dancing anymore. Hippopotamus stomped and thrashed about in the dark and felt the creatures bouncing off his body and head. The sound of the sticks and big pieces of wood crunching under his feet was so satisfying that it made him stamp even more. He was having so much fun stomping around that he hadn't even noticed that the screams and shouts of the little creatures had stopped and had stopped for some time, he just gleefully stamped around listening to the crunching in the dark until he was so tired that he fell asleep right where he stood.

The next morning when Hippopotamus awoke, he realised how hungry he was and so still half asleep he began to search for food. The caves around the circle were all empty and there wasn't any of the little creatures left hanging around so he started to eat up the scraps of meat that they had left lying around after they fled last night. He scooped up the meat in his giant mouth but found that it was full of bones and broken pieces of wood off of the floor but he was so hungry that he kept on eating anyway. He ate and ate until there was nothing left and his stomach was so full that all he could do was lay down and take a midmorning nap. It wasn't long however before Hippopotamus was being woken up. He could hear someone talking to him, still being tired and still being angry he growled at whomever it was trying to wake him but the voice did not go away. Hippopotamus tried to demand to be left alone but still the voice did not go.

"Hippopotamus" the soft voice called out like a doting mother trying to wake her baby from a nights' sleep. "Hippopotamus" it called out again, "you need to wake up, you need to see what you have done".

Hippopotamus could not ignore the voice and so he started to stir, but, as he started to come around, he could not see anyone there. "Who is there" he shouted "who dares wake me" he continued angrily but no one answered. As he started to lay back down the voice reappeared.

"Hippopotamus, I am very disappointed in you" this time the soft nurturing tone was gone and replaced with a much sterner one. "Look at what you have done!" This woke Hippopotamus up again and he was soon on his feet, this time he noticed where the voice was coming from.

Three tall figures stood in a beam of the morning sunlight, similar to the animals that he had scared the night before but much larger and Hippopotamus knew who he was addressing.

This was one of the gods, every living thing knew of the gods, knew that they were the creators of everything, even the mighty Hippopotamus and now, one of them was talking to him.

"Your temper has led you down a dark road!" it bellowed down to him. "You have done something that we cannot

forgive, your aggressive nature has cost us deeply!"
Hippopotamus knew he should not talk but felt the words
come out as though someone else was saying them.

"I did nothing wrong!" he exclaimed, "these animals
attacked me, I just wanted them to leave me alone and they
attacked me".

"Lies" the gods shouted back "You entered their home to
try to force them away, you could have walked away and
they would never have even known you existed".
Hippopotamus could hear the anger start to grow in their
voice and with it the anger in himself started to bubble up.

"I do not walk away" he screamed "I am the mighty
Hippopotamus." A sense of power and pride filled his voice
and made it boom out just as well as the voice of the gods.
"They should fear me, they should run from me, all
creatures should run from me" he began to stamp his feet as
he spoke. "The deer lied about me with that fawn, they

killed it not me, they tried to blame me. Then the lions ganged up on me when I tried to speak to them. Next the monkeys threw things at me and now these creatures attacked me with their pointed sticks. And you come to me and call me a liar. Where were you when I needed help, where were you when they did all of this to me? Nowhere! Even you hate me so why should I care that I scared a few little insignificant creatures away?"

The gods looked upon him, their anger had been completely removed from them, Hippopotamus could see the sadness in their eyes.

"But you did not scare them away" they said in a soft and saddened voice. "They never had that chance" their voice was filled with sadness almost like someone trying to hold back a tear. "You may be unaware of the consequences of your actions but when you nudged the little one away to scare them you killed them and then you trampled their fire and whilst they could not see to run you crushed them all one by one. You have taken them away from us, these beings that we gave life so that they could protect all living things and your anger has taken them away".

Hippopotamus was stunned by this. What did they mean he had crushed them? He replayed the nights' events in his mind. Their screams were gone and he'd had fun crushing their pointy sticks that was all. He turned away from the gods and started to walk back towards the edge of the circle where he had nudged the little one.

"I barely touched it" he murmured to himself "I only nudged it away to frighten it." Having reassured himself that he had done nothing wrong he turned back to the gods. "If I have crushed them all, then where are they?" he asked inquisitively.

"You ate them" they replied "this morning when you hadn't woken properly, you scooped them up in your giant mouth." The temper had completely disappeared from the gods' voice now, but Hippopotamus could still feel the disappointment in their tone.

"I ate the food that they left behind" he replied his voice still full of its conviction.

"No, my dear Hippopotamus, you did not. They left nothing behind because you made sure that they never left" the gods voice trailed off at the end as though they were deciding what they should do with him but Hippopotamus was not about to wait to find out.

"They should have left me alone; they all should have left me alone. Why won't you all just leave me alone, then I'll be happy and you can all be happy pretending that I don't exist." And with that he ran away.

He charged back up the hill and through the trees where the monkeys had thrown things at him the day before. When he reached the trees, he saw that they had returned and were sat around in the tops of the trees eating their lunch.

"I'll show those naughty monkeys" he growled to himself in a low tone and he barged into one of the trees that they were sat in. The tree shook so much that the monkeys began to slip and one by one they came tumbling out of the tree. As they fell Hippopotamus stood under the tree his huge mouth wide open and as they came crashing down, he swallowed them whole.

Then he ran off again, shouting and laughing about how he had got the monkeys this time and how they would not throw things at him again. He ran and ran further from the gods. He ran and ran back the way he had come from before, back towards his tree, his home and where this had all began. He ran all night and all the next day and was soon back in front of the abandoned home of the deer.

"I'll show those lying deer" he shouted as he smashed through their homes one by one laughing to himself the whole time. Off he went again towards his lake. Night had started to fall by the time he crossed the plain and he saw the lions asleep around a large rock.

"I'll show those mean lions, ganging up on me." He started to sneak up on the pride carefully taking one quiet step after another until he was stood right in the middle of the group. "Oh look" he whispered to himself "the lions have me surrounded" and with that he stamped down as hard as he could on the tail of the largest lion.

The largest lion began to howl in pain which caused the other lions to wake up startled, but before they knew what was happening the mighty Hippopotamus was stamping around on every tail he could see before he ran off back to his lake. With his two days of revenge done Hippopotamus settled down to sleep under his tree, a giant smile across his giant face as he drifted off to sleep.

The next morning when Hippopotamus awoke with blurry eyes, he wandered from the shade of his tree his eyes not yet adjusting to the morning light, down to the lake edge and with a giant yawn he jumped into the lake to wake himself up. However, to his surprise, he did not splash into the water but instead created a big cloud of sand that half buried him as it came crashing down. The sand had the same affect that he had hoped from the water, in so far as it woke him up, but it had not been as refreshing as he would have liked. Startled and confused he turned and ran back to his tree, all the time his feet slipping in sand. When he reached his tree however, he was not greeted by its large trunk and cooling shade but instead by a small green trunk covered in spikes that offered little to no shade at all.

"You wanted to be alone" the soft voice of the gods came from behind him. "You said we should leave you alone, so here you are"

"What is this place?" Hippopotamus demanded angrily. "Where am I?".

"You are in the desert" they replied, still in their soft and nurturing tone. "There is no place on earth where you can be more alone than in the desert" they proclaimed. "You can finally get what you have always wanted, solitude". With that the gods vanished and Hippopotamus was left all alone in the middle of a giant desert, with nothing but a prickly tree and sand as far as the eye could see.

Lost in the desert

How we handle punishment is a choice. We can rise above it and learn from our mistakes or we can rebel against it, often making things worse for ourselves and those around us.

Hippopotamus was not happy, which is understandable since he went to sleep under his favorite tree and awoke in the middle of a desert and he wanted everyone to know about it. He stamped his giant feet and roared with all his might. But no one was around to hear him. He charged about first one way and then back the other, but still there was no one to be seen. He ran towards the sun and then away from it but still nothing. Half the day was gone and all Hippopotamus had accomplished was he was now hungry, thirsty and tired, but still he had no one to complain to.

By the time the sun was gone and the night had fallen Hippopotamus had all but given up on finding anyone and was now beginning to realise that he had not seen any water either. This desert was nothing but sand and the one prickly tree.

"I must cross the desert" he mumbled to himself in a sad and weak tone, "I must find the water so I can get a drink in the morning" and with that he closed his eyes and tried to go to sleep. Hippopotamus had spent the whole day looking for anyone to talk to but he had not seen anyone, however as soon as he closed his eyes, he was awoken by strange noises coming out of the darkness.

"Who's there" he cried out, but no one replied. "Show yourself" he shouted again but still there was no response. The noises continued through the night, but no one ever replied as Hippopotamus continued to call out. Just before the start of the new day all the noise stopped and by the time the sun rose, the desert was quiet again and Hippopotamus felt that he was all alone once more.

Hippopotamus now knew that he wasn't alone but he also knew he did not have time to go hunting for anyone again today, he knew he needed to find water soon and eventually food. The noises would have to wait. So off he set, with the sun on his back he began walking away from the prickly tree in search of water. Slowly he went, his giant feet slipping into the deep sand, the hot morning sun burning his back but still he walked on.

As the sun rose in the sky and began to descend again the mighty Hippopotamus still walked on with the now dwindling sun light on his now burnt back, he walked further and further from the prickly tree but still he could see nothing that looked like water or food and still he had seen no signs of anyone that had been making all that noise the night before.

Another night fell and Hippopotamus needed to rest and so he laid down on the hot sand and started to try to sleep however, as soon as his eyes were closed the noises began again and again just like the previous night no one replied to Hippopotamus's calls. The third day in the desert was much the same, as was the fourth and even the fifth. Walking with the sun on his back in search of water and nights spent crying out to whomever was making the noise when the sun went down. The only difference was that his back was now completely burned and his feet were beginning to blister from spending his days walking across the hot desert sand. On the sixth day he didn't have the energy to keep walking the burns on his back had become so painful that it hurt to move which was fine by him as the blisters on his feet had begun to burst and bleed and so he lay there, on the hot sand, sobbing gently all day and well into the night.

As the night fell on the sixth day, the noises started up again but this time Hippopotamus did not care, he did not care if there was anyone around as he was too tired and in too much pain to get up and search the darkness for them and so he stayed put and as the sand around him began to cool he feel asleep with his tears still staining his huge cheeks.

"Hello" a quiet voice squeaked out to him. "You there, hello" it came again. The voice was so quiet and soft that Hippopotamus didn't even stir.

"I don't think it can hear you" squeaked a second voice "You'll have to shout" the second voice spoke out, with a sense of authority.

"Hello!" yelled the first, but still Hippopotamus didn't wake. "Well that didn't work, anymore ideas?" the first voice could hardly hold the contempt from its voice

"Maybe you should do the shouting, you are better at it than I am".

"Well that's because you keep giving me reasons to practice dear." The second voice spoke with an unmistakable hint of sarcasm in its voice. "Together" it commanded and both the tiny voices screamed as loud as the could in unison, "hello!" Hippopotamus heard them this time and began to stir. "Quick its awake" the second voice squeaked and the two of them began scurrying around in front of Hippopotamus waiting for him to wake up.

His eyes were still blurry from all the dried tears as he tried to open them, but as they adjusted to the moonlight, he could start to focus on who was talking to him. Standing a few feet away was a couple of small rodents covered in fur with giant ears, well giant for someone the size of a rodent.

"Who are you? What are you? Were you the ones making all that noise? Why did you wake me? What do you want?" the questions just flowed out of him one after another without any pause for them to try to answer.

The two were taken aback, they had not expected quite so many questions and were both just looking, first at Hippopotamus and then at each other. Back and forth they went as though they were waiting to see what happened next.

The second of the two rodents started to speak first. "Well I am Eugenia, and this is my mate M".

"Marty, the names Marty" the first rodent interjected with a hurried tone much to the disdain of his mate "and we are friends, well we would like to be your friend, we saw that

you were sad and wanted to see if we could help, that's
what we do, we help, or at least we try to help, we like to
help, don't we Eugenia, we like to help it's what we do" his
excitement was beginning to get the better of him and
Eugenia began to pull him back.

"Yes dear" she told him, in a voice that showed
Hippopotamus that this was not the first time Marty had
gotten like this. Then she turned her attention back to
Hippopotamus. "What my mate is trying to say is that we
saw that you were upset and wanted to introduce
ourselves."

"And to help" Marty shouted over her shoulder.

"Yes, and to help. If you would like it" she said the last part
through gritted teeth and was facing Marty the whole time
as she said it.

Hippopotamus knew that if he wanted to say anything to
these two that he would have to find the time whilst they

were talking to each other, like now, so he blurted out the same questions again only this time he missed out who are you? Emphasizing the what are you? Part of his enquiry. The conversation took a while as Marty often got carried away and started talking about what had come into his brain at that moment rather than the answer to Hippopotamus's questions but Eugenia was always there to reel him back in and to answer what she could of his questions. By the morning they knew all about the Fawn's death and how they had all held him responsible, and how the furless apes attacked him and yet the gods punished him and not them and Hippopotamus had learned that they were fennec foxes and they told him that they lived underground to avoid the midday sun and how they came out at night for food when the sun was gone and the sand had begun to cool.

"But I do not fit underground" he proclaimed when they told him it was the best way to avoid burning in the hot daytime sun.

As the sun began to rise, they showed him how the sun moved across the sky and how that had meant that he had not been walking straight all this time. They even took the time to show him how he could hide from the sun and to find water under the desert sand. Both of which required Hippopotamus to dig a big hole to climb in but because his feet were all blistered and sore, they decided to dig a hole for him, one big enough for him to fit in.

The next day was more comfortable as he hid in his hippo hole. But still he had nothing to drink or eat and as the sun went down Marty and Eugenia came back out to see him. They spent the night showing him how to find water but he still could not dig with his blistered feet and so the two of them did it for him again, they opened up a small puddle for him, as quick as they found it for him, he greedily drank it, the puddle was gone in one gulp of his great big mouth.

Over the next few days Eugenia and Marty returned again and again to show him how to find water and to help him dig a new hole and day after day his blistered feet stopped him from doing much of the work himself however, after a week of coming by, his two new friends did not show up. Hippopotamus spent the night patiently waiting for them to come and help him get something to drink but they never did. Day after day, and night after night he waited, but still they did not show up. Hippopotamus stayed in his hole until he could not bear his thirst anymore and so went out to find his friends. He walked through the dark shouting their names but no reply ever came and by the time the sun started to rise he realized that he did not know where his hippo hole was. So, he started to dig but as he dug down further the sand just slid back into the hole and he wasn't getting anywhere and by the middle of the morning the sun was so high that he could not hide from it even in the little hole he had managed to dig.

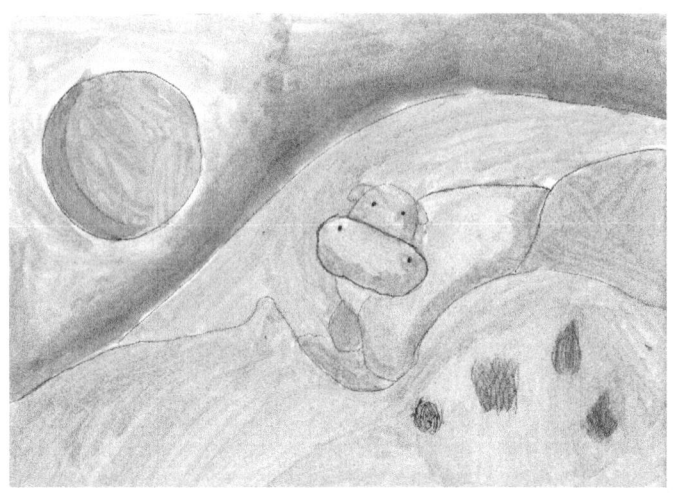

He lay in the sun and his skin was soon burning again and as the next night fell, he tried to dig for water but he could not clear the sand away and by the time morning had returned he still had nothing to drink and nowhere to hide from the sun. Another day passed and Hippopotamus could feel himself burning even more. His skin began to get so burnt that it started to bleed.

"Why have they abandoned me" he cried. "They said they were my friends" his tear-filled sobs broke up the words as he spoke them. Why would they stop coming? He thought to himself if they truly were his friend, they would not abandon him in his time of need.

"You never really cared about me" he shouted "You want me to burn" his sobbing started to fade and the anger he had once felt for the deer had returned. "Well I don't need you" he growled "I don't need anybody" he stood up as he shouted as though he wanted everyone to see who was addressing them "and I never did"

"Ha" came a squawking laugh from high above him, and as he looked up, he saw a flock of birds circling over-head and as he stared up at them, they all started to copy with the laughter until Hippopotamus's ears were ringing with the noise. The birds flew high above Hippopotamus's head for most of the day just laughing at him whilst he stood below them shouting back at them.

"What's so funny?" he bellowed up to them but they just continued to laugh. With each taunting hackle he grew more and more enraged. However, no matter how much he screamed they did not answer him instead they just flew in circles high enough that he could not reach them and yet low enough that he could hear them laugh. Even though Hippopotamus was as angry as he had ever been, the fact that he could not channel his anger towards anyone meant that he soon began to run out of energy and he flopped down to the floor trying to fight back the tears that were beginning to form in his eyes.

Hippo finds himself truly alone

Like a coin, a story always has two sides but unlike a coin which remains a coin when it is flipped over, when a story is flipped, we cannot so easily tell what it once was.

As Hippopotamus lay there completely defeated and so short on energy, he felt himself falling asleep and for the next couple of days he did not move, he did not search for water or try to hide from the sun, he just lay there, slowly burning, slowly dehydrating and with the birds still circling overhead. It was during the third day that one of the birds decided to land, not right beside Hippopotamus but just close enough and it started to hop towards him. Carefully watching for him to move as it did. But Hippopotamus did not move at all. So, with greater confidence the bird hopped closer still, slowly at first but more hurriedly with each step until it was stood beside the giant beast.

It started to peck at his side and still he did not move so it started to peck harder trying to break through Hippopotamus's thick flesh. The other birds saw this and flew down around him and immediately started to peck at his tough flesh but this was enough to make Hippopotamus wake and he was quickly trying to shout at them but his voice was too raspy. He tried to swing for them but his joints were too stiff and so the birds began to flock back around him and stood there watching him.

"What do you want?" he croaked at them "Why are you trying to eat me?" his voice was low and his words labored but he knew they understood him. Yet, silently they stared. "Why are you doing this to me?" he yelled.

"Because it is what we do" the response came from the first bird that had landed "this is our curse" he continued on. His voice seemed to trail off at the end of each sentence. "We only get to eat what has already died" he said dreamily almost as if he didn't want to waste his energy on talking.

"What do you mean curse?" Hippopotamus asked his head finally rising up from the floor. With this new found show of energy most of the birds took flight. And as he started to move more followed but the first bird that had answered him stayed where he was. "What curse?" he asked again but the bird just stood and watched him as though he was studying him. After a short silence the bird started to answer.

"You are here" he said as though that should have answered Hippopotamus's question but when it realized that he still did not understand it continued "the gods sent you here" it said followed by another studied pause "we were all sent here as punishment for what we did wrong when we lived in the green lands".

"But I did nothing wrong" Hippopotamus responded.

"Then why were you punished?" the bird enquired "You must have done something".

Hippopotamus started to tell the bird all about the fawn and how they blamed him and how the furless ones had attacked him with sharp sticks. The bird just stood in front of him and listened until Hippopotamus had finished his story.

"May I tell you our story?" the bird asked. "Maybe it will help you to understand" the bird just stood still and waited for Hippopotamus to respond but when he just sat there in silence the bird started to tell its story anyway.

"We are vultures, and we live on the flesh of dead animals. But we are weak, we cannot fight, we cannot hunt, we" the vultures voice trailed off to the point that Hippopotamus could not hear what it had said.

"Go on" he pleaded

"Weak, we are weak" the vulture repeated "and so we had to scavenge for food." He took another pause here and just watched Hippopotamus a little longer but just as he was about to speak the vulture started again. "Now I'm sure you know what a lion is, don't you?" Hippopotamus was about to answer but the bird did not give him the time "of course you do and I am sure you have seen them eat; they don't really leave much when they have done."

"So, you attacked the lions?" Hippopotamus asked with the enthusiasm of a child.

"Oh no" came the vultures reply "we stole their food" a hint of pride flashed through the vulture's voice. "They had it and we wanted it so we took it."

"What's wrong with that" exclaimed Hippopotamus "I always took what food I wanted"

"Nothing" replied the vulture "that's the circle of life, the problem was we got greedy with it and we starved the lions out until they became our food too"

"What a brilliant idea" Hippopotamus replied "but surely that's part of this same circle?"

"It is" the vultures chest puffed up as it spoke "but the gods did not see it that way. We ate all the lions in the green land and this meant that all the other animals flourished".

"Again, surly that's a good thing, a part of the circle?".

"It was, but all of these new animals ate all of the grass and the trees until nothing was left but dirt. Then they all started to die too. There was never more food available for us at this time. We no longer needed to steal. This is where the gods stepped in".

"What did they do? Did they send you here just for eating what you were made to eat?" Hippopotamus's enquiry seemed to be full of rage. "They punished you for surviving".

"Not quite" the vulture replied "we were not sent anywhere, they just commanded that we stay on the green lands even though the green was gone. And with it all the animals were gone and soon the dirt turned to sand and the world around us began to heat up. We were not sent to the desert we created it." The vulture stopped here to give Hippopotamus time to comprehend what he had said. "We created this arid land through our greed and it was our punishment to stay here without food or water. But then, they started to send other animals here as punishments so we got our food back anyway. That's why we are happy to stick around unlike the rest of you."

"They can't all be bad, what about Eugenia and Marty?"

"Who?" the vulture replied.

"Eugenia and Marty, they were a couple of fennec foxes. They were nice. Well, until they abandoned me that is."

The vulture started laughing again "you, you mean, you mean that couple of foxes that you worked to death?" he could hardly get the question out through the laughter. "They were sent here because they were selfish, they used to hoard food, hide it away from anyone that tried to get anything to eat. The gods punished them because they refused to share".

"What do you mean worked to death, they offered to help me, to show me how to find water" Hippopotamus gasped as he forced the words out. "I never forced them to do anything".

"You didn't know? You thought they had run off because they were tired of helping you? The gods sent them here because they were selfish, they believed that if they helped others the gods would let them leave. Turns out" the vulture began laughing again "Turns out their punishment was helping you to death".

The laughter of the vulture had drawn the attention of the other vultures who had all landed around Hippopotamus without him realizing, that was until they all burst out laughing too.

Hippopotamus could hear them all chuckling to themselves and then he realized that they were whispering also.

"He was friends with the foxes" he could hear a few of them saying and a few more replying inquisitively "the ones we ate before we found him?" and it became painfully apparent that his friends hadn't abandoned him.

"Why do you blame me?" he asked with a tear in his eye

"Because every time they found some water you gobbled it all up" the vulture replied. "That was their curse they had to help everyone until they met someone more selfish than they were."

With the deafening sound of laughter behind him Hippopotamus began to run, his head held down he did not care how tired or thirsty he was he only knew that he needed to get away from these awful birds and the awful things that they were saying about him.

Day and night, he ran, further and further across the desert but he did not stop and he did not slow down. That was until he stumbled across a familiar sight. The prickly tree, where he had been left by the gods, was right there in front of him when he looked up. Somehow, he had found his way back and he knew that it was the gods' way of reaching out to him and with that a sense of relief washed over him.

When Hippopotamus reached the prickly tree, he threw himself to the ground where he had first awoken and he closed his eyes as tight as he could, tight enough to hurt his face as he did and he started to cry. These were not the tears of someone that has been hurt or done something wrong but the tears of someone that just wants you to listen, wants to be heard. He knew in his heart that the gods were listening to him and that they were waiting for him to return. However, no matter how long he waited no one came. He still waited and each day he began to mutter to himself that he would behave, if they only let him go home, he would behave himself, but they still did not come. After a while he started to add new pleas into his daily ritual, first he added that he would help the deer find out who had hurt the fawn, then he added that he would talk to the lions about why they attacked him and finally to the monkeys for

bashing them out of their trees. But still no one came.

Hippopotamus makes a realisation

Punishments are so effective because we hold ourselves responsible, when we learn to accept what we have done and truly forgive ourselves we can no longer be punished in our heart.

After many days and many nights Hippopotamus began to fear that the gods would in fact not come to see him, that they had abandoned him here. He did not understand why though, surely, they could forgive him was that not the point of a god. One night when he had finally stopped waiting for the gods to arrive and resigned himself to his fate, he heard a whisper in the darkness. Too faint to make out at first but as it neared him it became clearer to him that it was two voices talking to each other. The soft voices of Eugenia and Marty. Hippopotamus opened his eyes excitedly, happy that his friends had returned and that the vultures had been wrong but they were not there. Their voices had gone quiet, replaced by nothing more than the wind rustling through the sand and so, although slowly at first, he closed his eyes so that he could drift back off to sleep. However, no sooner had he closed his eyes the voices started again.

"Typical, this lazy Hippopotamus just lying there whilst we do all the work" whispered Marty.

"Quiet we don't want to wake him" Eugenia replied with her usual sharp tone "Let's get some of the water for ourselves first.

Hippopotamus slowly opened his eyes again and could just make out the silhouette of his friends but as he opened his eyes wide, they once again disappeared.

After a short search he once again settled down, convinced that he had heard and seen his friends and yet confused that he could not find them. This time however he did not hear the pair when he slept. Instead, he heard the laughing of the deer playing in the lake. He could hear their screams of excitement and the splash of the water as they kicked and leapt about, he could even feel the spray of the water gently rub across his face. Yet, as he opened his eyes, he was greeted by nothing but sand.

Again, he slept and again he heard the fawns playing, felt the water splashing, only this time he could feel himself running but no matter how hard he tried he could not open his eyes. Hippopotamus felt himself leap into the air, towards the lake just as he had done so long ago, but this time was different. This time he could see the fawns in the lake beneath him, he could see the look of terror in that one fawn's face as he came crashing down. He woke up violently shaking, tears flowing down his face.

"I did it" he cried out "I didn't mean to do it" his tears became whaling sobs "It was an accident" but now he could hear himself laughing, he could feel the joy as he played, as he accidentally crushed the tiny fawn. Now he knew why the deer had feared him. He could feel his anger the same as he had that day when they all judged him and remembered racing off to confront them. He knew he was still in the desert but he could feel his body charging forward, his memory was so clear now that he could see the lion cubs up ahead but he did not care that they were sat eating their breakfast and he felt them crashing against him as he barged through the group of cubs, trampling their food as he passed.

Next, he came to the trees and could feel himself shouting up at the birds and crashing through their trees their nests falling from the high branches as he ran past. He remembered seeing all of the birds taking flight as he shouted up at them.

Finally, having witnessed him smashing through the trees and frightening the birds and knocking down the nests. He reached the home of the deer but they had left already and, in his rage, he smashed their homes and started back the way he had just been. He felt that he was mad at the deer for leaving and so he started to run home without a thought of what was going on around him. Before he had not realised that the nests had fallen out of the trees and that they now littered his path and as he returned, he could now hear the sound of snapping twigs and eggshells crumbling under foot. Back at the lion cubs he could see that all the lion mothers had banded together and were stood in front of their injured cubs. Hippopotamus knew what had happened now he had hurt the cubs and destroyed their food in his rage and with this realisation he could feel himself beginning to cry again. He had hurt so many without realising it.

"I am sorry" he whimpered "please forgive me".

This time however, his pleas did not go unheard or unanswered. The gods had been listening and had finally come to him.

"You see, this is who you are" they told him "you hurt those around you without thought or concern" their words cut like daggers and Hippopotamus began to cry even more.

"Please forgive me" he cried out "please let me go home."

"Why should we?" the gods asked in reply. "We sent you here so that you were alone as you had requested, we sent the Fennec foxes to show you that you needed friends and you did nothing more than take advantage of their generosity. You only cry now because your back is burnt and you have nothing to eat and no water to drink."

"Can't you see how upset I am?" he proclaimed "Can't you see that I have learned my lesson?" Hippopotamus's tears began flowing even faster than before. So fast, that they began to pool on the floor beneath his massive head.

"Not really, no" they replied to the sound of

Hippopotamus's whaling growing louder. "You have

realised that you were wrong but we find it hard to believe

that you have changed. We find it hard to see that you are

not the same Hippopotamus that you have always been"

their words hurt Hippopotamus deeper than he ever thought

possible. "What about the world of man? you trampled

their village to the ground and ate every last one of them

and deep down you were happy whilst you did it."

Hippopotamus knew that this was also true, was he really the bad one? Did he really enjoy bringing misery to others? The pool of tears beneath him had grown, as he had cried more and more as the conversation continued. Now it had broken the banks of its original puddle and had begun to flow down to the bottom of a small basin in the desert and it had begun to form a much larger puddle. The more the gods spoke of his past deeds, the more they told him he had not changed the more the tears flowed until this second puddle had formed a small lake in the desert.

"There now you have somewhere to swim, some water to cool yourself off with" the gods told him.

"But I still have nothing to drink" he replied, "I did not learn how to dig for water, I am not as good as my friends had been and I did not learn how to dig a hole properly when they tried to show me" his usually strong frame looked weak as he pleaded with them some more. "Please let me come home" he tried one last time but the gods did not want to hear his pleading anymore and they disappeared just as quickly as they had arrived.

Hippopotamus had once again found himself alone, only now he had his new lake to swim in but as he tried to stand up he realised that his skin was completely burned, every inch of him hurt as he forced himself up to his feet and as he started to walk towards the waters' edge he realised that he had been lying still in the sun for days and his body was too tired to remain stood for long. He splashed into the lake but as it had been made by his tears the water contained to much salt and it was impossible to drink so he just lay in the water throughout the entire day letting its cooling embrace wash over him.

The night time was too cold to stay in the water though, so Hippopotamus had to come out and lay on the sand until he fell asleep. The night was filled with noises again, just like it had been before he met Marty and Eugenia and he felt a little bit of joy bubbling up inside of him at the prospect that he might see them again, even though deep down he knew they were gone. As he lay asleep however, he got the familiar feeling of water splashing across his face, he thought about everything he had done before, expecting to relive it as he had done on previous nights but this time, he saw nothing. Then came the squeaking sound of small voices and another splash across his face, this time however, it was enough to wake Hippopotamus up and to his surprise, he saw a group of small rodents playing in the water just in front of him.

They did not see that he was awake and somehow did not hear his groans as he pushed himself up. Hippopotamus was so hungry, he could not remember the last time he ate something and was, in his tired and sleepy state, about to scoop up the first of the rodents when one of them yelled out.

"What are you doing?" the angry voice of one of the rodents came from beside him "we are not food" it yelled again and in his startled confusion he let the rodents escape. Once they were gone and the night had fallen silent again, he collapsed to the floor.

"The gods were right; I have not changed" his voice quivering as it approached tearful again. For the rest of the night he lay there, perfectly still and trapped in the moment between self-reflection and self-doubt. However, as he woke in the early morning sun, just as he was about to slip into the water again, he noticed that the prickly tree that he had once laid beneath, now had a beautiful flower near its

top.

Now Hippopotamus thought to himself, at least he had

something to look at as he splashed around throughout the

day and as another night fell, he lay back down and drifted

off to sleep. more noise came with the next night, and just

as they had done the night before the rodents came back for

a swim, only this time as he woke to the sound of them playing, he spoke before he moved.

"I am sorry for last night" he called out to the darkness, but at first, he got no reply, "I am sorry that I tried to eat you I was just hungry as I have not eaten in ages."

"Eat that tree then" came the soft voice of one of the rodents.

"I can't it's too prickly" he replied.

"On the surface it is but when you dig a little deeper it becomes soft and smooth."

Hippopotamus listened to them playing for a little longer before he made his way back to the prickly tree.

"Tomorrow" he whispered to himself "Tomorrow, when I can see what I am doing" and with that he settled down for another night's sleep and this time it truly was a peaceful night's sleep.

Hippopotamus's new friends

Through our trials we can learn to show ourselves for who we really are, whether that is for the better or for worse we are finally free to show our true colours, Hippopotamus had been through many trials in the desert and now it was time for him to find his true self.

With the dawn of a new morning came a new sense of belief for Hippopotamus, the rodents had informed him of how to get food from his prickly tree and this was exciting news for him. Without a thought of anything else he leapt to his feet and, with his new sense of determination, began to franticly dig beside the tree. Just as the rodents had told him, the spikes disappeared as he dug deeper. It wasn't long before Hippopotamus could get his mouth around the base of the tree and with his mighty teeth, he began to pierce holes in the trunk. As his teeth punctured the base of the tree a rush of water spurted out and straight down his throat, the coolness of the water was instantly refreshing to the tired and weary creature and he began drinking it as fast as he could. It was not long however, before the tree had no more water to give and Hippopotamus was still thirsty so he punctured more holes in the tree to try to find more water but none came and soon the tree was full of more holes than it had spikes.

Hippopotamus sulked off away from the tree and as the sun had begun to rise and the day was growing hot again, he slid into the lake so that he could stay cool. It was at this time that he realised that he was alone again, all of the

rodents had gone and there was no noise apart from the

occasional rustling of the sand by the wind. Hippopotamus

huffed and mumbled under his breath, with no idea of what

he could do to keep himself entertained he just lay in the

cooling water and drifted off back to sleep. For hours

Hippopotamus just lay there, in the sun, completely

submerged except for his eyes, his nostrils and a small spot

on the top of his back completely at peace with his little

world, a silent world that was only broken by the

occasional snore and grunt filled yawns.

As the day slowly drifted into night the silence was once
again broken and the desert began to come alive, as the
rodents returned for another night by the lake. They were
shocked when they first arrived for Hippopotamus was still
snoring away in the lake and not under his tree as he
usually was, but the gleeful and playful rodents did not care
that he was asleep and were soon jumping into the water,

enjoying its refreshing coldness and playfully splashing around together.

Hippopotamus woke up startled and was about to shout at the rodents when one of the youngest of the group swam right up to his nose and looked straight into one of his massive eyes.

"He's awake" he shouted gleefully "everybody looks, he's awake" and with that all the other rodents came swimming across to greet him. One by one they shouted out, their greetings getting louder and louder as they tried to out shout each other.

"What's going on?" he mumbled, his voice muffled as it was still under the water. "Why are you all shouting?" this second question was louder as he rose his head from the water and began to take stock of his surroundings. But as he spoke louder the rodents just screamed and shouted their greetings over the top of his bellowing voice.

It wasn't long before Hippopotamus found himself just trying to get away from them all and was just about out of the water heading back towards the prickly tree when he heard the voice of the one that had spoken to him the previous night.

"Please don't go" its squeaky voice pleaded "they are all just excited to see you."

"Why?" Hippopotamus replied, the inquisitive and confused tone was easy to pick up on "I tried to eat you" he continued.

"Who hasn't" the rodent replied "we are small enough that everyone tries to eat us at some point" his voice still seemed to be filled with excitement and joy as he announced this to Hippopotamus. "If we didn't speak to anyone that tried to eat us, we would only be able to speak to ourselves and how boring would that be?"

Hippopotamus found himself nodding in agreement with the little rodents' words, he had wanted to be alone for so long that he hadn't thought about how boring it is to only have yourself to talk to.

"But why now? Why today? You were not like this yesterday" he asked.

"Because yesterday we did not know we had you to thank for this lake" the rodent replied and as he did the rest of the rodents joined in to a chorus of thanks to the Hippopotamus for making the lake. "It's the only one in this whole desert" he said, his voice full of pride "and you let us come here and haven't tried to scare us off, it's rare to find someone who isn't selfish around here, everyone is being punished for something, I'll bet even you, but you're the only one making it a better place."

Hippopotamus was taken back by this comment, how was he making it a better place he wondered to himself, he was responsible for the death of the fennec foxes and spent his days paddling around in the lake. He had never even thought of doing something for anyone else.

"I did not make this lake though" he said "who told you that I made the lake?"

"The vultures" the rodent responded; Hippopotamus could hear the contempt in his voice. "They said you cried it into existence because you felt bad."

"Why did you say it like that?" Hippopotamus asked.

"Like what?" the rodent replied.

"With that tone in your voice."

"Because the vultures seemed happier about your misery than they were about the miracle that you performed" his answer took Hippopotamus by surprise.

"Miracle?" his voice trailed off, as though he was trying to understand what had been said.

"Well, what else would you call it? You brought water to

the desert and with your kindness you got a flower to

bloom, they sound like miracles to me" and before

Hippopotamus had time to reply the rodents were all back

off in the water playing together, laughing and splashing

around. Hippopotamus just lay at the side of the water

watching his new friends playing every so often laughing

as one of them did something silly or crazy and for the first

time since he had been sent to the desert, he found himself

enjoying life, he found himself to be happy. He realised

that it was because for the first time he wasn't alone.

As the night drew to a close and the sun began to rise the rodents began to say their goodbyes to him before they all started to run back off into the desert, one by one disappearing from view until there was only one that remained.

"See you tonight?" it asked half knowing the answer and as Hippopotamus began to nod enthusiastically, the last of the rodents ran off into the desert, calling back one last time as it went "and don't forget to eat the prickly tree" it shouted as it too vanished into the desert.

Confused, Hippopotamus began to walk over to the tree, he had not thought about eating the tree the day before, when he punctured the trunk, the rushing water had made him forget all about actually eating the tree and so as tired as he was he went over to eat the tree. To his surprise when he arrived the base of the tree was buried again, as though he had never dug it up before and so he began to dig the sides out once again, the trunk of the tree was undamaged as though he had not bitten it the night before and as Hippopotamus began to bite there was a rush of water and he drank the clean water from the tree once more, only this time he took a huge bite to eat out of the side of the tree, before he slid back into the water, to spend another day asleep in the lake.

The next few days were the same as the last, Hippopotamus slept through the day and was awoken by the sound of the rodents playing. They played all night as he watched them and then as they departed in the morning, he went back to the prickly tree to find it was full of water again. After about two weeks of this the numbers of rodents began to increase as more and more of them became aware of the lakes existence and it wasn't long before they began to over fill the lake. More and more kept arriving and soon the noise was unbearable to Hippopotamus and he found himself hiding from them as they arrived, his peaceful lake had become a playground for what seemed like every rodent in the desert. For the first time since his tears had formed the lake, he felt that he was going to cry. He had liked the fact that the rodents looked up to him and he didn't want to lose that by scaring them away now, there was just no room in the lake for him anymore. They had taken over completely. He patiently waited for the morning to come as that was when the rodents would leave and he could have his lake to himself once more. The next day as the sun rose however, the rodents did not leave. Instead they stayed, they continued to play all day long and soon, as the sun reached its highest, Hippopotamus could feel his skin begin to burn again. Enraged he stomped down to the lake side and roared as loud as he could.

"Get out!" he yelled his voice echoed throughout the entire desert. "Get out of my lake" he screamed again but the rodents did not listen to him. This angered Hippopotamus more than anything ever had before and he was just about to dive in the water and force them all away when he saw the young rodent that had been staring him in the eye all those nights ago, only now it was not moving. It was motionless in the sand at the side of the water, its little chest barely moving as it took small and laboured breaths. Hippopotamus's rage was all but gone and he opened his giant mouth and scooped up the defenceless creature with his tongue. At this all the rodents froze in fear; the mighty Hippopotamus was about to eat the youngling and they would probably be next. However, Hippopotamus did not bite down, instead he turned and ran back to the prickly tree where he frantically dug the sand from its side and tore open the trunk with his giant teeth, the tree fell down as he ripped and tore away at it, not even caring that the spikes had been stabbing him in the face. As he reached the bottom of the tree he gulped the fresh water into his mouth and let it wash over the poor little rodent. He could feel the little one wriggling around in his mouth as it drank the water and as it did its movements became larger and faster until, after it had had its fill, it leapt from his mighty mouth and back down to the desert floor. Without a single word, not even a thank you, the rodent ran back to the others and they scurried off into the desert, instantly leaving Hippopotamus alone.

Hippopotamus just crashed down onto the floor, the realisation of what had just happened and the fact that his face was now full of spikes and that his prickly tree was destroyed, the tears that he had felt coming earlier started to flow once more.

Hippopotamus cried for two full days and two full nights and in this time, there was no sight or sound of the little rodents. With his face so sore and with no prickly tree to drink from Hippopotamus just sulked the days away. It wasn't until the third day that he heard anything, the squeaking of one of the rodents waking him from his daze, however, as it approached, he noticed it was different, its back was covered in thousands of spikes.

"Sorry" the quiet voice of this new creature was instantly recognisable to Hippopotamus; it was the youngling he had saved. "We didn't mean to ruin your home" it continued "and I should have thanked you for saving me rather than running away." It held its head down as it spoke, its nose seemed to disappear under the shell of spikes and Hippopotamus felt as though it would just roll away if it wasn't careful.

"It's okay" he said trying to sound reassuring and sincere. "But what happened to you?" he had tried not to say anything but his curiosity had gotten the better of him. "How did you get covered in spikes?"

The rodent looked up at Hippopotamus as though it was confused by the question, but soon began to talk.

"We were punished by the gods again; we were sent here originally because we have a nasty habit of taking over things that don't belong to us and we did it again with your lake. The gods decided that we needed to be punished again as our actions led to you getting stabbed by that prickly tree and so they gave us these spikes to remind us of what we did to you" Hippopotamus had never heard someone speak with so much remorse and was instantly taken back by it.

"I didn't want this for you" he told the rodent "I was happy to share my lake with you, until you took up all the space."

"Well I'm here to make it up to you the best I can" the tiny rodent proclaimed and with that it walked over to him and began pulling the spikes from Hippopotamus's face.

When the job was done and all the spikes had been removed the tiny rodent began to walk away back towards the desert but stopped as Hippopotamus shouted after it.

"Will you come back? Will you all come back to play tonight? I miss the laughter."

Without any response however, the little rodent disappeared into the desert and Hippopotamus was once again left alone. Unsure if his friends would return and unsure what the gods had planned for him and what they

wanted from him again.

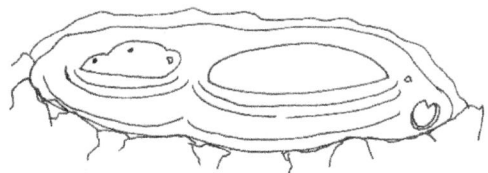

The river guardian

We see the world the way we believe it to be, sometimes we need to stop looking at the world in our usual way and start to appreciate the stories of those around us.

Hippopotamus now knew he didn't want to be alone anymore and he had to find a way to see the world as others did, to find his place within it.

It had been a few days since the little rodent had pulled the spikes from his face and yet Hippopotamus still woke up at the start of every evening waiting for them to come back to the lake and each evening he lay there alone, not even a sound came out of the desert, as though the wind had also abandoned him. Night after lonely night he sat back waiting, morning after morning he slid into the water and cried himself to sleep. The prickly tree had since been covered by sand but this seemed to be the only movement in the desert. Hippopotamus was back where he had started, no food, nothing to drink and no one to talk to, he knew something had to change. So, on one evening, as soon as the sun set, he began to walk away from his lake. For half the night he walked away and for the second half he returned to his lake to stay cool, but no matter how far he walked and no matter in which direction he went he did not hear a single sound. It was hopeless he thought to himself and after a couple of weeks, hungry, thirsty enough to consider drinking from the salty lake and sad that he was still all alone he started back towards his lake. Saddened and depressed he marched with his head pointed down to the floor, barely high enough to be able to make out his own footprints, he trudged back towards the lake. When he neared the lake, he heard the sound of someone laughing.

Hippopotamus's heart bounced as he charged excitedly towards the noise and just before he reached the brow of the last hill before the lake, he saw the vultures all standing around, with their backs towards him, so focussed on what they were looking at that they did not notice this gigantic Hippopotamus bounding along behind them.

"Back again?" he yelled as he approached, loud enough that they all jumped up startled and began to fly away. "You're not eating me" he yelled out as load as he possibly could but the vultures just turned to him lazily and in their dreariest of voices each proclaimed in turn.

"We aren't here to do that."

"Then what are you here for?" he yelled at them.

"To work out how you did it" they replied in their usual

dulcet tone. Hippopotamus was just about to ask them what

they were talking about when he reached the top of the hill.

To his surprise the rodents were back at the lake playing,

but not only that, they had returned with some new animals.

Birds with long legs and long necks. Deer like animals with

strange horns and a taller animal with a huge hump on its

back. But the strangest thing was that they seemed to have circled his lake and were drinking the salty water.

All of the animals were laughing except for the vultures who seemed particularly angry about them all playing in the lake. As he approached, he noticed that the edge of the lake had changed also, it was no longer surrounded by sand but rather had a grass bank and the prickly tree that had disappeared under the sand had returned and was now larger than it ever had been before. Excitedly Hippopotamus ran down to the side of the lake, never had he been so happy to see so many animals around and as he approached them all they greeted him like they already knew him.

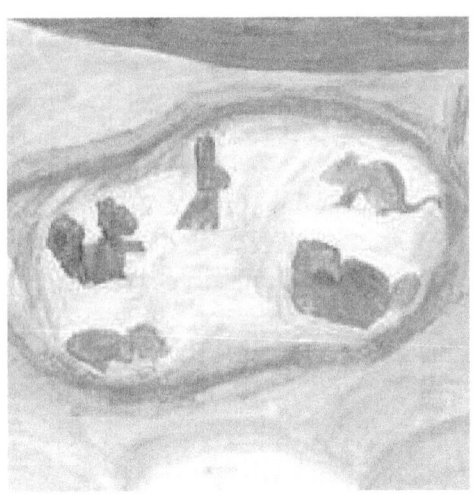

The youngling started to walk over to Hippopotamus as soon as he saw him with a big smile on his face.

"You said you didn't want to be alone" he cheerily yelled as the two of them reached each other. "I thought that you would like to meet some of the other animals of the desert." With that he turned around and ran over to the large birds to introduce him to them, and then the two of them spent the rest of the evening and the start of the next day chatting to each and every animal that had arrived, they talked about the things that they had done wrong to get put into the desert and how they had heard of the magical lake that the Hippopotamus had cried into existence.

"But how are you drinking it?" he asked them "it is far too salty". They just laughed at him.

"This water is the freshest we have ever tasted." Came the reply, and so, Hippopotamus, cautiously, went down to the waters' edge and took the smallest drink he could manage, expecting it to be salty, but it wasn't the water was clear, and it was fresh, as fresh as the water had been that he used to get from the prickly tree. Upon tasting how fresh it was he took a giant gulp and carried on with his meetings, until he was sure he had met every animal at the lake edge. All the animals continued to play and dance and laugh, all through the next night and well into another day before any of them started to leave and the whole time the vultures just sat and watched from atop the hill.

"Why don't you join us" Hippopotamus called up to them, but when they did not answer he tried again, this time walking over to them. "There is plenty of space, and plenty of water for you all to join us." But still they did not move.

He tried again and again to get them to tell him why they did not want to be a part of the group but they always seemed reluctant to hear him. Finally, after what felt like most of the day talking to a group of vultures that said nothing in return, he started off back to the waters' edge looking back over his shoulder as he went.

"The invitation is open" he yelled back "you can come and join us anytime."

The next few days saw more and more animals come to the lake, day and night they came. Some for a drink before they headed back off, some to gather around and play and some even came just to sleep in the water next to Hippopotamus. Never before had he felt so popular but still the vultures just sat back and watched. Their judgemental glare never moving from the group, no matter what time of day it was at least one of them had an eye keenly focussed on Hippopotamus whatever he was doing.

"Why do the vultures keep watching you?" one of the rodents asked him one evening, "do they not like you?" but Hippopotamus had no answer. He had tried to talk to them but they never responded, they just stood there watching him. Judging him. He did not care though, for the first time since he arrived in the desert, maybe even for the first time in his life he was happy, he was smiling and laughing and he knew that it was because of the other animals that spent their days around him and he wasn't about to let a few vultures ruin it for him.

Days quickly became weeks and then months and Hippopotamus was finally happy he hadn't even focussed on the vultures in weeks when one of them finally spoke.

"We have been watching you" he announced as though this was supposed to be news to Hippopotamus "we have been waiting" his voice seemed laboured as though he was almost too weak to talk. "Waiting for you to get back to your natural state, waiting for you to attack everyone. You are a bully; you always have been a bully and you always will be a bully."

Hippopotamus felt himself getting angry at the vultures, how dare they call him a bully, how dare they treat him this way. He could feel the rage building up inside but before he acted on it, he thought back to his first dealing with the vultures. They had been happy to be punished here, they had been happy that the gods had sent others here to be punished and it was not his fault that they wanted everyone to be as miserable as they were.

"Think what you will" Hippopotamus told them "I am not like that anymore; they are my friends and I won't ever do anything to hurt them or anyone else anymore." His words must have meant something to the vultures because as soon as he had said them, they took flight and disappeared off into the distance. Hippopotamus never saw the vultures again.

That night as he fell asleep and all the other animals had gone, he heard someone approaching, their soft steps almost completely silent and undetectable, had it not been for the eerie silence of the desert night. As they approached he heard them begin to talk to each other and instantly recognised their voices. Marty and Eugenia.

"Well done Hippopotamus, we are proud of you" they exclaimed, and he could hear the sincerity and pride in their voices "you did what we couldn't. you actually made a difference to the world; you actually made a change in yourself" and with that they drifted off as though they had never been there before. Hippopotamus drifted deeper into his slumber until he was finally shaken awake by the voice of the gods.

"Rise young Hippopotamus, rise up and tell us of this new land that you have created."

Hippopotamus was a little confused as he had not created this land at all they had and he started to tell them as much when they interrupted him.

"Were they not your tears that made the lake?" they asked.

"Yes, but..." he started to reply.

"And was it not the lake that drew the hedgehogs to you?" their questioning continued.

"Yes" his answer was more precise than before as he expected to hear them ask their next question but continued when he thought they were not going to "but I did not tell them of it."

"And did you not help the little one when he needed it" there question seemed to ignore what he had said previously.

"Yes" he started to answer only to be interrupted again.

"Even though in doing so you hurt yourself and destroyed your one water supply."

"Yes" he answered again "but he was my friend and he needed help."

"You invited them back also?" this question seemed more like a statement but their brief pause told him that it was a question that he should answer anyway.

"I did."

"Even though they destroyed your home, you invited them back anyway."

"Yes" said Hippopotamus, "because I didn't want to be lonely anymore, but I didn't make the lake stay, I didn't plant the tree or make the new one grow, I didn't plant the seeds for the grass or stop the water from being salty. I can only assume that you did all of that."

"That is correct" the gods told him "we rewarded your good behaviour with the niceties of life. Your sorrow made the lake so how could we take that away from you. Your selfless act of sacrificing your tree for another planted the green seed back beneath the sand and your compassion to all of these amazing animals is what gave you the next tree." Hippopotamus could feel the sense of pride growing inside of him as the gods spoke but he did not speak himself instead, he just sat back and listened to them as they continued.

"And even when you were provoked by the vultures, when they told you that you were a bully, you rose above the anger that you felt and left them to be themselves. That is what we had hoped for you" this last sentence took him by surprise and Hippopotamus could not keep quiet when they said it.

"What do you mean hoped?" he shouted back at them "You sent me here to punish me" he could feel himself getting angry with them.

"We did" they replied in a very matter of fact kind of manner "however, it was only ever to serve as a lesson, a warning of what life holds for you if you act this way again. Have we not made it clear that bad things happen to bad people and good things come to those that are good?"

"That doesn't make sense" replied Hippopotamus. "The fennec foxes were not bad, why did they need to be punished" he asked.

"They did not get to leave because they made a false change. Their actions were not about helping others but about trying to prove they were better. You did not try to prove anything when you saved the young hedgehog."

"And there is the second one, these, hedgehogs, why cover them in spikes they did not deserve that" Hippopotamus shouted out angrily.

"Their actions led to the destruction of your home as well as causing you physical pain" the gods reply took Hippopotamus by surprise. How could they be so cold to these little rodents, especially the young ones.

"And what about the vultures, they haven't changed and yet they were not punished" finally he believed that he had caught them out but they replied just as readily.

"Their punishment was that they got to watch the rest of you thrive and have fun, they were happy here until you made your little oasis and all the animals flocked to your side and thrived with the fresh water."

Hippopotamus could see that the gods spoke the truth and was just about to thank them until they spoke one last time.

"Now we must leave" they said and Hippopotamus felt sad that he could not ask them all the questions that he had. "There is no room for you here anymore and you now need to return home, back to the plains" there voice told Hippopotamus that there was no use fighting them and he began to shed a tear for all the friends that he would have to leave behind.

"But there will be some changes from now on. Firstly, you will live in the great rivers and not your tiny lake as you did before. Secondly, you will only come out at night to feed so that the other animals can feel at ease around you. Thirdly, you must not eat any more meat so as not to eat anyone by mistake. Lastly, you must protect the smaller animals as best you can, you must let them feed from you and keep them safe. This is your new life as the river guardian."

With this final word the gods were gone and Hippopotamus felt himself fall into a deep sleep and when he woke up the next morning he was no longer in his oasis but instead, found himself at the side of a mighty river surrounded by trees and animals and not a grain of sand as far as his eyes could see. The gods had been true to their word, he was home.

Printed in Great Britain
by Amazon

34114658R00068